and the
Lost Library

written by Anita Nahta Amin

illustrated by Farimah Khavarinezhad
and Marta Dorado

raintree
a Capstone company — publisher

T0372086

Raintree is an imprint of Capstone Global Library Limited, a company incorporated in England and Wales having its registered office at 264 Banbury Road, Oxford, OX2 7DY – Registered company number: 6695582

www.raintree.co.uk
myorders@raintree.co.uk

Edited by Aaron Sautter
Designed by Elyse White
Original illustrations © Capstone Global Library Limited 2025
Production by Whitney Schaefer
Originated by Capstone Global Library Ltd

978 1 3982 5720 7

British Library Cataloguing in Publication Data
A full catalogue record for this book is available from the British Library.

Acknowledgements
We would like to thank the following for permission to reproduce photographs: Shutterstock: farres, 65, Kandarp, 7. Design elements: Shutterstock: Hulinska Yevheniia, inspired-fiona, Lera Efremova, LeshaBu, Pattern_Repeat, Redberry, Tartila, Timmy Tayn, Veronique G, Witthawas Suknantee

Contents

Hiya, it's Reeya!

I'm Reeya Rai! My Hindu family is originally from India. My parents are archaeologists. I love to go along on their adventures all around the world!

Me with my parents!

My robot, Tink!

I also love to invent things that help my parents with their cool discoveries. I invented Tink! He's pretty useful to have around.

Finlay is a whizz with computer code and electronics. He helped me program Tink! His parents are archaeologists, too. They work with my mum and dad.

 Elsie and her dad, Dr Acker

Elsie is definitely NOT a friend. She's bossy and spoiled. Her dad, Dr Acker, is a rival of my parents. He's jealous of their work and often turns up whenever my parents make a big discovery.

Hindu Culture

Hindu homes are often filled with large families. Grandparents, parents, siblings, uncles, aunts and children often share a home. The home may be passed down through many generations. Elders, not just a parent's siblings, are called "auntie" or "uncle" to show respect.

Hindus remove their shoes before entering a house or temple. The streets outside are considered filthy with germs and dirt. Shoes are removed to prevent tracking dirt and germs inside.

Beef is forbidden in a strict Hindu meal. Many Hindus don't eat meat at all. Hindus believe that cows are holy because they give milk, which can sustain life. They do not hurt or kill cows. Cows are often allowed to roam freely in towns and villages.

Karma is one law of Hinduism. Hindus believe that if you are good, good will come to you. If you do something bad, you will receive something bad in return.

Dharma is the law that tells Hindus how they should behave. It teaches them to be kind, patient and honest, among other virtues.

Words to know

achha good

beti daughter

haveli mansion

kyaa what

ruko stop or wait

shukriyaa thank you

haveli

Chapter ①
The hall of statues

On her first day in Egypt, Reeya had hoped to spend a lazy day at the beach. But instead, she and her best friend, Finlay, found themselves staring into a deep hole in the rocky sand. A rope ladder dangled to the ancient catacombs below, where their archaeologist parents were working.

Reeya's dad shouted up to them. "Just climb down slowly. You'll be okay!"

Reeya didn't like heights – or the dark. But she wanted to help her parents, so she forced away her fears.

Mum and Dad need Tink, she proudly reminded herself.

Tink was a toy robot she and Finlay had built together. Her parents wanted to use it to explore the catacombs. Reeya thought inventions could solve most problems, including archaeological ones. She especially loved it when her inventions could help her parents.

Reeya pushed up her glasses and told Finlay, "I'll go first."

"Okay," Finlay said with relief.

Afifi, a young archaeology student, clipped Reeya into her safety harness. Then she slowly climbed down the shaky ladder. "It's not too bad," she shouted to Finlay when she reached the bottom.

After Finlay climbed down, Afifi lowered a basket that held Tink and a laptop computer. Reeya lifted Tink out of the basket while Finlay picked up his laptop.

"Okay, make sure you stick close to me," Dad told them. "The other tunnels have never been explored. They may not be safe."

As they walked, Reeya held up her lantern to look around. The tunnel's massive stone and plaster walls took her breath away. They were covered with sea blue and rust-coloured murals of people and animals.

"These designs remind me of the homes in India," Reeya told Dad. India was her grandparents' homeland. Many of her relatives still lived there. Reeya remembered the colourful designs on their *haveli* walls.

Dad agreed. "Yes, Egypt and India have a lot in common. They were ancient trade partners. That's why we're here. This town was an old seaport. It's possible sailors from India came through here."

"So, are we looking for sailor artefacts?" Reeya asked, ducking through a tunnel with a low ceiling. "How would a boat get in here?"

Dad smiled. "We probably won't find any boats. We think sailors used this place to rest, sell things and bury their dead. So, we might find treasures like spices, linens, bones, books–"

"What kinds of books?" Finlay interrupted. "Will we get to see an ancient graphic novel?"

"It's possible," Dad said. "Or something similar. The Great Library in this town had thousands of books from all over the world. Whenever a sailor docked here, they had to give their books to the library. The library would keep the original. But they made a copy on papyrus to give to the sailor."

"Can we go to the library?" Reeya asked. She loved libraries and had spent countless days researching invention ideas there.

"No. We can't, unfortunately," Dad said. "It burned down more than 2,000 years ago in a war."

"The library burned down?" Finlay repeated, horrified.

"What happened to the books?" Reeya asked, equally horrified.

"Most people think the books burned too," Dad answered. "But some people, like myself, think some books were rescued and hidden somewhere to keep them safe from the invaders who set the fire."

Reeya remembered her grandfather once telling her that books held knowledge and should be respected. Many of her relatives believed it was bad luck to step on a book. She asked, "Do you think the books will ever be found?"

"I hope so," Dad said as they joined Mum and Finlay's parents. They were standing next to a pile of rubble that blocked the tunnel. In the rubble was a hole that was too small for a human to fit through. But it was just large enough for a robot to slide through.

Mum smiled. "We're ready to send Tink in. We think there might be statues in there!"

Finlay's mum strapped her video camera and torch to Tink. Then Reeya placed Tink into the hole's opening. Finlay pressed a button on his remote control to move the robot forward.

A video of the tunnel flickered to life on Finlay's computer screen. Everyone watched intently. Soon, Tink entered a chamber beyond the rubble. They all gasped. The chamber was lined with soapstone statues. One of them was of a boy with a monkey on his shoulder.

"He's our age!" Reeya exclaimed.

She noticed that hieroglyphs were carved into the base of the statue. The symbols started with a viper and ended with a chick. Reeya remembered that Mum once said hieroglyphs were an ancient Egyptian language.

"What does it say?" Reeya asked.

"I can tell you," Finlay said eagerly. "I installed a program on my computer that translates hieroglyphs." He ran the program over the video. A few moments later, a name flashed across the screen – Vishnu.

"Vishnu is a Hindu name!" Dad said. "We need to find out more about him."

Reeya wondered why the statues were there, especially the one called Vishnu. Why had he come all the way from India to Egypt? And most of all, what made him important enough to have his own statue?

Chapter ②
The boastful tale

For the rest of the day, Reeya and Finlay sifted
through buckets of rubble looking for tiny
artefacts. But they found nothing interesting.
They were glad when Dad finally said, "Great job
for today. Let's stop here. My back hurts."

As they trudged down the pavement towards
their rented houseboat, Reeya squinted in the
outside light. It was cloudy, but it was still brighter
than in the catacombs.

As they passed a shipyard, Reeya waved at a
man hauling wood and poles from an old boat to
a scrap pile. He bowed gently back towards her.

Then Reeya noticed a group of people climbing out of colourful rowing boats. Some of them wore diving gear. But then Reeya saw one blonde girl who wore a frilly pink swimming costume, sun hat and sunglasses. She was carrying a bucket.

"Oh no. Look over there," Reeya said, grabbing Finlay's arm and pointing.

"Huh? What's Elsie doing here?" Finlay spluttered. Elsie was the daughter of Dr Acker, an archaeologist who worked for another museum. Reeya and Finlay didn't like Elsie much. She had a habit of being very selfish and rude.

"I have no idea," Reeya replied. "But let's hurry so she doesn't see us."

Reeya and Finlay tried to hide behind their parents. But Dr Acker had already spotted them and was heading their way.

"Hello! I'd heard you were in Egypt!" he bellowed. "I was invited to teach at the local university here. But for a bit of fun, we're searching for the remains of the Great Library. We're close to the sea, so it's probably underwater, don't you agree?

"So . . . what's it like in those stifling catacombs? Have you found anything?" Dr Acker's beady eyes swept over them greedily, as if planning to snatch any treasures they might be hiding.

Before anyone could reply, Elsie huffed. "Can we go? I'm tired. I had to spend all day at that school before we could finally go to the ocean."

"Sea," Dr Acker corrected.

Elsie rolled her eyes. "Whatever. At least I found a cool rock by the beach. But now I want to go back to our room."

"Well, we'd better not delay you," Mum said quickly. "We're tired too. Have a nice evening."

"Until next time," Dr Acker said, looking annoyed as he led Elsie away.

Later on the houseboat, as the sun was setting, Reeya finally got to relax on the deck. Mum sat in the chair next to her. Together, they watched the palm trees swaying in the fresh sea breeze and the nearby boats bobbing up and down.

"Will you tell me a story?" Reeya yawned, snuggling under a blanket.

"Okay, *beti*. How about a tale from the *Panchatantra*? Do you want to hear the one about the boastful turtle and geese?" Mum asked. The *Panchatantra* was a book of old Indian animal stories.

"Yes, that's my favourite!" Reeya said, settling in to listen to Mum tell the story. She laughed at the funny ending as she always did. "How did the author even think of that story?" she asked.

"I don't know," Mum said. "Nobody knows who wrote it. Experts think it was written about 2,000 years ago, but the original manuscript is missing."

"Do you think we can find it?" Reeya asked.

"Maybe one day," Mum said.

After a while, Mum reached over and turned on the radio on the table. She clicked through the channels until she found one that was in English. The announcer was talking about the weather. Reeya sat upright when she heard a broadcaster say, "Severe Weather Alert".

The voice on the radio continued. "The storm is expected to bring heavy rain and dangerous flooding in three days."

Reeya gasped, realizing the catacombs where they were digging could be flooded too. The water could damage the murals and statues, including the statue of Vishnu. All of her parents' hard work would be ruined! She had to find a way to help protect the catacombs.

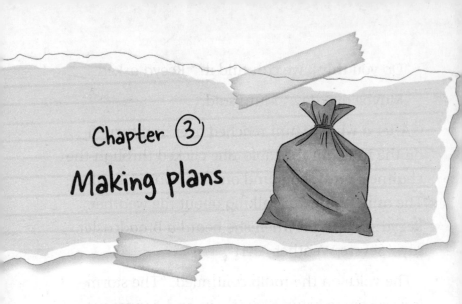

Chapter ③
Making plans

Everyone on the houseboat gathered around the radio and listened closely to the weather forecast. The coastline and streets were all expected to flood.

As the parents started planning, Reeya scanned the sky. Was it just her imagination, or were the clouds already getting darker?

"We'll need to cover the shaft to the catacombs really well so water doesn't leak in," Mum said.

The adults decided to cover the catacomb shaft with tarps to make it waterproof. Then they'd place wooden planks on top of the tarps to hold them down and keep rainwater from seeping in. Finally, they'd set up a wall of sandbags around the shaft to help keep flood waters away.

"You two can help me pick out supplies at the timber yard tomorrow," Dad told Reeya and Finlay. "We have tarps, but we'll need to buy the other items. I'll ask Afifi to come too. He can translate between English and Arabic if needed."

"Will this houseboat be safe in the storm?" Reeya asked as the boat gave a sudden leap on a rough wave. She almost lost her balance.

"She's right," Finlay's mum said. "It won't be safe. We need to move to land."

"We'll check if there's an inn available tomorrow," Finlay's dad agreed.

With a plan made, they all went to bed, but Reeya didn't sleep well. She hoped everything would go smoothly. But as an inventor, she knew from experience that plans didn't always go as expected.

* * *

The next morning, Reeya, Finlay, Dad and Afifi took the tram to a maze of outdoor shopping stalls. At first, Reeya felt overwhelmed. There were large crowds of customers, bright colours, smells, music and shopkeepers trying to sell them something at every turn.

"This reminds me of the bazaar in India!" Reeya exclaimed.

"Yes, me too," Dad laughed.

Afifi led them down streets of various shops filled with lanterns, spices, perfumes and fake artefacts. After dragging Finlay away from a fez shop, they arrived at a timber yard, where long wooden planks were stacked high.

Dad approached a carpenter and said, "Hello. We need to buy a few supplies. We need wood, sandbags and nails." After Afifi translated, the carpenter led them around the timber yard, recommending supplies.

Reeya and Finlay helped measure the wood and sandbags. The shaft measured three metres long and two metres wide. Reeya calculated the amount of supplies needed to cover the shaft and build a wall at least five sandbags tall.

"We'll need 120 sandbags!" Reeya exclaimed.

"That's a lot of sandbags," Dad said. He ordered the supplies and asked the carpenter, "Can you deliver them?"

"He'll deliver them tomorrow," Afifi translated.

"But he won't be able to carry them all the way to the catacombs. He has too many other deliveries to make. He'll need to leave them on the side of the road for us."

Dad frowned. "So, we'll need to carry the supplies from the road to the shaft? That's a lot of bags to carry, but I suppose we have no choice."

"We could buy empty sandbags and fill them on site," Afifi suggested.

"That's a good idea," Dad said. "But that will take a long time. I'd rather spend that time sealing the catacombs."

As Dad paid for the supplies, Reeya frowned. She wanted to find a way to help carry the sandbags to the shaft, especially with Dad's sore back. She blinked quickly, thinking of an idea. She knew what to do – she'd invent a supply transporter!

Chapter ④
The transporter

At the catacombs, Reeya and Finlay brainstormed how to make the supply transporter. They stood at a crate they were using as a table. A tape measure snaked between them. They had just measured the distance from the road to the catacomb shaft.

Reeya pulled out her notebook and a pencil. "Let's list what the invention has to do. It has to move supplies twenty seven metres over rocky sand. It has to support the weight of the supplies, and it must hold different sizes and shapes of supplies." She spoke as she wrote.

She remembered Dad had said the sandbags weighed about eighteen kilograms and the wooden planks weighed about thirty kilograms. She wrote those weights in her notebook too.

"What if we make a bigger, stronger version of Tink?" Finlay asked. "It can pick up the supplies and carry them to the catacombs."

"That would be cool," Reeya answered. "But I don't think we'll find the parts for that kind of robot here. We don't have much time either. We need something that works by tomorrow when the supplies get dropped off."

Finlay agreed. "That's true. It'll be hard to find a motor too, so it can't be electric."

Reeya nodded. "Right. The supplies will need to be pulled or pushed. Or moved by gravity." Gravity made her think of a slide at a park. But she knew friction could cause the sandbags to get stuck and stop on a slide.

While thinking about how to solve this problem, Reeya fidgeted with her pencil, rolling it back and forth across the page.

Suddenly her eyes grew wide. The rolling pencil gave her an idea. "We can make a slide with rollers!"

Reeya quickly sketched a diagram of the slide and labelled the parts. She explained the drawing to Finlay. "Gravity will pull the sandbags down a slide. But they might get stuck along the way. Instead, we can use rollers to keep the bags rolling forward."

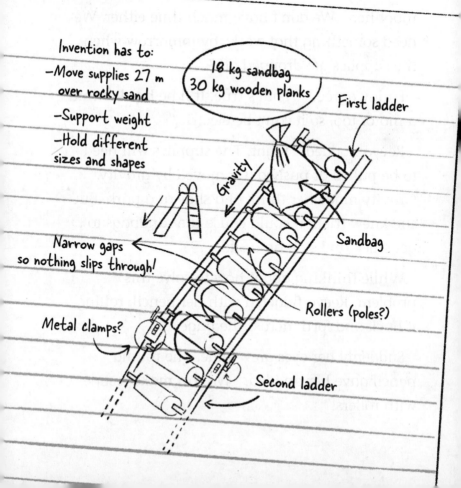

Invention has to:
—Move supplies 27 m over rocky sand
—Support weight
—Hold different sizes and shapes

18 kg sandbag
30 kg wooden planks

First ladder

Gravity

Sandbag

Narrow gaps so nothing slips through!

Rollers (poles?)

Metal clamps?

Second ladder

"That's a great idea!" Finlay agreed. He studied Reeya's sketch. "So we need rollers, a frame to hold them and something to support the frame."

"Exactly," Reeya answered. "Let's go and find the parts."

As they looked around, Reeya saw some ladders lying on the ground. The rungs reminded her of rollers. "We could connect these ladders together to make the frame, take out the rungs and put in rollers."

She measured the length of the ladders. "There are enough ladders here to reach from the road to the shaft," Reeya said.

"We could raise one end onto that crate," Finlay suggested. "That will angle it like a slide. But where do we get the rollers from?"

"Hmm, that's a good question." As Reeya checked around, she noticed a tugboat pulling an old boat out on the sea. The old boat reminded her of the shipyard. "The shipyard has poles in their scrap pile. I saw them yesterday when we went by there. Maybe the man working there will let us use them."

Reeya calculated how many rollers they would need for each ladder by counting the number of rungs. She wrote the number down in her notebook.

"We just need to make sure the rollers are spaced correctly so nothing falls through the cracks."

Reeya told Mum about her idea and asked to use the ladders. After Reeya promised to put the ladders back together afterwards, Mum let Reeya and Finlay go to the shipyard with Afifi.

The shipyard was busy with people working all around. The place smelled of freshly painted boats and musty sawdust. Reeya and Finlay found the scrap pile and saw a man sawing wood. When Afifi tapped him on the shoulder, the man shut off his whining saw.

"Hello, can we have some of your scrap poles?" Reeya asked politely. "It's to save the ancient catacombs over there from the flood that's coming." She pointed in the direction of her parents' site as Afifi translated.

The man studied them. After a moment, he said something in Arabic.

Afifi said, "He said you can take whatever you like from the scrap pile. He'll cut it for you too if it helps to save a part of Egypt's history."

Reeya smiled. "How do you say thank you in Arabic?" she asked Afifi.

"*Shukran*," Afifi said.

"Shukran," Reeya smiled at the man. She thought it sounded like one of the Hindi words for thank you, *shukriyaa*.

The friends rummaged through the scrap pile to find what they needed. In a short time, they had gathered several long, thick wooden poles and some thin steel rods. "I think these will work," Reeya said.

It took all three of them to carry one pole. With Afifi's help, Reeya asked the man to cut each wood pole into equal pieces, and the steel rods into slightly longer pieces. She also asked the man to drill a hole through the centre of each wooden piece.

While the man sawed and drilled, they also found several metal clamps and bolts to hold the transporter together.

When they had all their supplies, they made several trips to carry everything back to the catacombs.

"Now we just need to build the transporter," Reeya said, crossing her fingers. She hoped nothing would go wrong.

Chapter ⑤
Let's roll!

Reeya and Finlay got to work making the transporter. One by one, they threaded a steel rod through each wooden piece to make the rollers. They grabbed a ladder and used screwdrivers to remove the screws and rungs. Then they replaced each rung with a roller. The ends of the steel rods fit through the nail holes in the ladder. They bolted the steel rods to the ladder with nuts and washers.

"Okay," Reeya said after making sure the rollers spun freely. "I think we should test this first part before we get too far and find out it doesn't work."

"Good idea," Finlay replied. He dragged the crate over to Reeya, and they leaned the transporter against it.

Reeya looked around and found Mum's satchel. While Finlay held the top of the transporter in place, Reeya dropped the satchel down the transporter.

Whir–Bunk. Whir–Bunk. Whir–Bunk.

Each spinning roller gently bumped the satchel down the ladder until it reached the ground.

"It works!" they cried together.

The two friends got to work converting the other ladders. Then they lined up the ladders end to end, from the road to the shaft. They fastened tight metal clamps around the ends of the ladders where they joined together. Now they had one long transporter.

"Let's give it a final test," Reeya said, picking up the satchel.

Finlay propped one end of the transporter up on the crate again. To help support it, they placed more crates and rocks under the frame. Then Reeya placed the satchel on the end. They watched the bag bump all the way down from the road to the catacomb shaft.

"YES!" The friends high-fived each other.

"Let's go and get our parents!" Reeya said.

When their parents had gathered around, Reeya motioned to the transporter and said, "Ta-da! Presenting the Egypto-Rollo-Transporter!"

"Wow!" Mum said. "What does it do?"

"Try it out, Mum!" Reeya said. She showed Mum how to drop her satchel down the rollers. The parents clapped and cheered when it landed.

"Amazing!" Finlay's mum smiled.

"This is great!" Finlay's dad said.

"It'll be a huge help for moving those supplies," Dad agreed.

As they waited for the supply truck, Reeya updated her notebook with details about how they built and tested the transporter.

Soon she heard the rumble of an engine, squeaking wheels, and a loud **Beep! Beep!**

She looked up to see a brightly painted truck parked on the road. In the back, piled higher than the truck, was a mountain of sandbags and wooden planks. It was all tied down with rope.

Reeya joined the adults and ran up to the carpenter. She showed him how to use the transporter. He frowned and shrugged, and then unloaded a sandbag onto it. When it bumped down the transporter and a crew member picked it up at the other end, the carpenter smiled with surprise.

The carpenter and adults unloaded the rest of the supplies, one by one, and sent them down the transporter. Sometimes the bags snagged, and Reeya had to get them unstuck and help them along. One wooden plank fell through the gaps between the rollers. So Reeya and Finlay helped carry it to the shaft.

Finally Dad said, "That was the last one." With everything unloaded from the truck, the carpenter waved and drove away.

"Many thanks to the Egypto-Rollo-Transporter. Your invention was so helpful," Mum told Reeya and Finlay.

The group then got busy preparing the catacombs for the storm. While the parents arranged the tarps and planks over the shaft, the crew got busy building the sandbag wall around it.

Finally, when all was finished, Mum gave an approving nod. "*Achha*. It looks good."

Lastly, Reeya and Finlay disassembled the transporter and put the ladders back together. Just before they all left, Reeya told Afifi, "Stay safe."

"You too," he said.

Reeya took one last look at the shaft. With the tarp, boards and sandbags, the catacombs seemed well-protected. She just hoped it would withstand the coming storm.

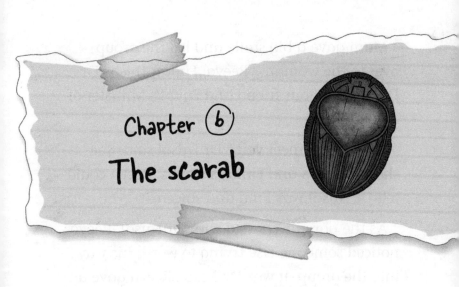

Chapter 6
The scarab

The next morning, Reeya's group moved from their rented houseboat to an inn on a nearby bluff. Fighting the wind, Finlay's dad managed to pull open the door of the inn.

"We were lucky they had room for us," he said as they entered the inn. "The innkeeper told me they've had a flood of customers trying to escape the storm."

Inside, the lobby was packed with tourists, local residents and other archaeologists. A woman wearing a hijab was surrounded by people trying to get her attention. When she saw Reeya's group, she smiled and waved.

Mum gave a big smile and led the group over to the woman. "Reeya, Finlay, this is Dr Faisal. She's our friend and Egypt's Minister of Antiquities."

"It's nice to meet you," Dr Faisal said. She shook Reeya's and Finlay's hands. Reeya could tell Dr Faisal was kind and sincere.

As the parents chatted with Dr Faisal, Reeya noticed someone else trying to worm his way into the group. It was Dr Acker. Reeya gave a silent groan. That meant Elsie was probably here too. Reeya looked around but didn't see her.

"I enjoyed your recent lecture about scarabs immensely, Minister Faisal," Dr Acker said in a charming voice. "It was one of the best lectures I've ever attended."

Reeya asked, "What's a scarab?"

"A scarab is a kind of seal," Dr Faisal explained with a smile.

"Oh, I visited California once and got to see seals there," Finlay said. "They were swimming and sunbathing and so cute. I didn't know there were seals in Egypt too."

The Minister chuckled. "Oh, no, that's a different kind of seal. The seal I'm talking about is something ancient Egyptians signed documents with. Scarabs look like a beetle on one side and have the owner's name or other special hieroglyphs on the other side."

As the adults moved on to other topics, Reeya and Finlay got bored and escaped to some seats at the other end of the reception. There was a coffee table there, and someone had their feet kicked up on it. The person wore flip-flops, and their toenails were painted a bright pink. Reeya quickly put her arm out to stop Finlay.

"It's Elsie," Reeya whispered.

Reeya started looking for somewhere else to sit when she glimpsed the blue stone in Elsie's hands. Elsie was busy studying the stone and hadn't noticed Reeya and Finlay yet. One side of the stone looked like a beetle. When Elsie turned it over, Reeya could see the other side was engraved with hieroglyphs. She recognized two symbols: a viper and a chick.

Reeya stopped and stared. Based on what the Minister had just explained, Elsie appeared to be holding a scarab. She remembered that Vishnu's statue in the catacombs had hieroglyphs that included a viper and a chick. Reeya wondered if Elsie's stone had anything to do with Vishnu.

Just then, Elsie glanced back over her shoulder. Seeing Reeya and Finlay, she quickly hid the scarab away in her pocket and narrowed her eyes at them. She kept her hand in her pocket as if guarding the stone.

"What are you doing? Spying on me?"

"No. We were just looking for a place to sit," Reeya answered, wondering how to ask to see the stone. "So . . . I happened to notice you had a cool souvenir. I'd like one too. Can you tell me where you bought it?"

Elsie smirked. "I didn't *buy* it, silly. I found it at the beach. And it's not a souvenir. It's a special ancient rock. It's probably the only one like it in the whole world. See?" She took the scarab out of her pocket and flashed it in front of Reeya and Finlay.

"Wow," Reeya said, sounding impressed. "I'll bet you get famous for finding it. Can we take a picture of you with it?"

Elsie's eyes lit up when Reeya said the word famous. "Umm, I suppose it's okay, as long as you don't touch it." She held the stone up next to her face so Reeya could see the hieroglyphs and gave a wide smile for Finlay's computer camera.

"Do you think I'll be in the newspapers?" Elsie asked through her smile.

"Maybe," Reeya said. "But if it's really old, it should be in a museum."

"No way. Finders keepers," Elsie argued, stuffing the scarab back in her pocket. She hurried away as if afraid someone would snatch it.

With Elsie gone, Reeya asked Finlay, "Can you pull up the hieroglyphs for Vishnu, the boy statue? I think they're the same as the ones on Elsie's scarab."

"Really?" Finlay quickly set down his computer on the table. He pulled up Vishnu's hieroglyphs on his screen, and they compared it to Elsie's stone.

The hieroglyphs matched. "Elsie has Vishnu's scarab!" Reeya exclaimed.

Chapter ⑦
The storm

Reeya studied the photo of the scarab on Finlay's computer and noticed more hieroglyphs etched at the bottom. When Finlay ran his program, they translated to New Mouseion.

Reeya frowned. "What does that mean?"

Finlay shrugged. "Maybe Vishnu helped mice?"

"Hmm," Reeya said. "We should ask our parents. They might know what it means."

They found their parents alone in the small library next to the inn's reception. Its shelves sagged with worn books. A vase of lotus blossoms sat on the centre table. The flowers reminded Reeya of India. Many of the lakes there were covered with similar flowers.

Reeya settled on a plush sofa and explained Elsie's scarab to her parents. When she told them about the markings on the scarab and how they were translated on the computer, Dad scrunched his eyebrows in a frown.

"The Mouseion was one of the greatest research centres of ancient times," Dad said. "It's where the Great Library was."

"Does that mean New Mouseion was also a research centre? Maybe a new library was built to replace the one that burned down?" Reeya asked, growing excited.

"It's possible," Mum said. "But remember, the scarab might be a fake. It may just look old. The lab would have to analyse it to be sure it's real."

"If it's real, Vishnu must've been very important to have his own seal. Maybe he was the head librarian or something," Finlay mused.

"Maybe," Finlay's mum said. "The library probably didn't let just anyone sign their documents."

"But he was a kid," Reeya reminded everyone. "How could he have worked for the library?"

"Even kids worked back then," Finlay's dad said. "Some were even kings or queens."

Reeya wondered what Vishnu's life had been like. Had he missed his family in India while travelling to Egypt? He would have been new in a different land with different customs and languages, much like her dad's parents had been. She hoped Vishnu had felt welcome here.

Reeya suddenly wondered about something else, and her eyes grew wide. "Wait. If Vishnu's statue is in the catacombs, does that mean that – the library might be there too?"

"That's what I was thinking. Either there or where Elsie found the scarab!" Finlay said.

"It's possible," Mum agreed. "Or it could be somewhere else – if it even exists. It's hard to know. But now we have another reason to keep exploring the catacombs when this storm is over."

As if on cue, the overhead lights flickered. Everyone looked around nervously.

BA-BOOM! Strong thunder made Reeya and Finlay jump in their seats as the inn rattled.

They tried to distract themselves from the storm. While Finlay played around with new computer code for Tink, Reeya pulled out her notebook and pencil. She tried to think of invention ideas, but her mind kept drifting back to Vishnu and the library.

She wondered if any of the old library's books had survived the fire. If they did, maybe they'd be in the new library now. She wanted to help her parents find the new library . . . assuming the storm didn't destroy it first.

Rain and wind thumped and crashed against the windowpanes. When the lights cut off, an inn worker came and put a lantern on the table. Before the worker left, she said, "Don't worry. This inn has been standing for more than 300 years. You're safe here."

But when Reeya peered out the window, she gasped. The road had turned into a river. She hoped her parents' work site, and the new library, wherever it was, weren't underwater too.

Chapter 8
A discovery

After the storm passed, it took several days for the flood waters to drain away and the power lines to be fixed. During that time, Reeya and Finlay desperately tried to avoid Elsie while they were stuck inside the inn. But one afternoon, Elsie cornered them.

"You told on me! I found that rock fair and square!" She seethed angrily. "But some government lady took it from me. And now my dad is angry. He said I embarrassed him!"

Reeya thought she saw a tear in Elsie's eye. For a moment, she felt sorry for Elsie. Reeya always wanted her parents to be proud of her too.

But then Elsie continued. "My rock got taken away because of you. So now you owe me."

"Hey, it's not our fault," Reeya protested.

"Hmph! We'll see about that." Elsie said, narrowing her eyes and stomping away.

Reeya was relieved when they could finally leave the inn. On the way to the catacombs, they passed damaged homes, fallen palm trees and smashed rowing boats.

The group worried about what they would find when they reached the site. Would the tunnels be full of water or collapsed? They navigated around puddles and windblown rubbish until they reached the site. Reeya saw someone familiar working.

"Afifi!" Reeya exclaimed and gave him a hug. She was glad he was safe.

"I'm glad you all fared well," Afifi smiled. "Some water seeped in through some cracks in the ground, but we're drying that now. Otherwise, there's no damage."

"That's great news!" Dad said. "Good work."

After the catacombs were dried out, the team went back to work clearing the entrance to the Hall of Statues. As the hole grew larger and larger, Reeya grew more impatient. When the last chunk of rubble was removed, Reeya leaped towards the hall.

But Mum stopped her. "*Ruko*, Reeya. Let's make sure it's safe first."

She walked into the hall carefully to check things over. Then waved for the others to come in. "I couldn't see anything that might cause the room to collapse. I think it's okay," she said.

"Where do you think the new library is?" Reeya asked, searching the walls. She was disappointed to not find a doorway.

"We'll know more after we take a scan of the hall," Mum answered. "The scan is sort of like an X-ray. It'll show us any spaces in the walls. The spaces might be other chambers."

While Mum set up her equipment and took images of the walls, Dad handed brushes to Reeya and Finlay. "You two can help by dusting the statues."

Reeya headed straight for the Vishnu statue. It was as tall as Reeya. She gently dusted the stone features and inscriptions, admiring the detailed artwork. She liked details. Through creating her inventions, Reeya had learned that even the slightest difference in detail could have a big effect on how an invention worked.

When she finished dusting Vishnu, Reeya felt a little disappointed. She hadn't found any new clues. There were no fake levers or hidden messages. So, she moved to the next statue. When she dusted its feet, she suddenly stopped and stared at the base of the statue. "Wait a minute . . ." She darted from one statue to the next, checking their bases too.

"Finlay, come look! All the statues are sealed to the floor with mortar – except Vishnu's," Reeya said excitedly. She got down on her belly to get a better look at the base of Vishnu's statue. There was a tiny gap between it and the floor.

"This statue sits on stone wheels!" Reeya called out. "You can just barely see them. Most of the wheel is inside the base."

Finlay got down next to Reeya to look too. "You're right! Maybe there's something underneath!"

"Let's tell our parents," Reeya said excitedly.

"Mum! Dad!" they yelled out, running up to their parents and grabbing their arms.

"We found something!"

"You need to see this!"

Reeya and Finlay talked over each other, trying to share their discovery.

"Whoa," Dad laughed. "One at a time please."

When Reeya told them what she found under the statue, the parents' eyebrows shot up.

"Really?" Finlay's mum said. She went over to the statue and knelt down to take a look. "My goodness, you're right! Let's try to move it and see what's underneath."

Working together, the excited parents started pushing the statue. The stone wheels clunked against the stone floor as the statue moved sideways.

The group stared in awe. Under the statue was a hole in the floor – with a staircase spiralling down into the darkness.

Chapter ⑨
The New Mouseion

"There must be something important down there," Reeya said. "Why else would it be hidden? I wonder if the library is down there?"

"Let me go down first," Mum said. "If it's safe, you can follow me. Afifi, can you set up a safety harness?"

Once the harness was in place, Mum strapped herself into it and slowly descended the stairs. Her lantern grew smaller and dimmer the further she went. When she reached the bottom, she shouted, "It's okay! You can come down."

Step by step, the rest of the group slowly climbed down the steep staircase. With her lantern held high, Reeya imagined Vishnu climbing down these same smooth stone steps thousands of years ago.

A dark and narrow tunnel waited for them at the bottom. They followed the tunnel through a doorway cut through the rock.

Their mouths dropped open at what they saw. Before them was a large chamber lined with stone shelves. Hundreds of rolled-up old scrolls filled the shelves. Wooden chairs with seats made of linen cord were scattered around the room.

Reeya tilted her head and studied the murals on the ceiling. They showed a burning building and people fleeing with books. One of the people appeared to be a sailor with a monkey on his shoulder. The people looked familiar. Reeya realized they looked just like the statues in the chamber above – and the sailor was Vishnu!

Suddenly it all made sense. "Not all of the books in the Great Library were destroyed in the fire. These heroes were able to save some of them and store them here!" Reeya exclaimed. "This must be the new library – the New Mouseion! And the Hall of Statues must be to honour the heroes."

"You're right! This is the New Mouseion," Finlay said, holding his computer towards an inscription in the ceiling. "That's what those hieroglyphs say, according to the computer program."

"But why hide the new library?" Reeya wondered aloud. "Books are for everyone."

"Invaders were known to burn books," Dad explained. "So maybe the entrance was hidden to protect the books."

They surveyed the fragile yellow documents. Some were crumbling into fragments. Others were still intact with pieces of string tied around them.

"Most are written on papyrus scrolls," Finlay's dad observed. He was taking notes and already planning on how to protect the manuscripts.

Reeya noticed one manuscript that looked different. It had thin sheets that were stacked, not rolled. And the sheets were tied together with string through holes in each one.

"What about this one?" she asked.

Finlay's dad took a look. "These are dried palm leaves. That's what people from ancient India used."

The writing on the leaves looked like the ancient Sanskrit texts that Mum sometimes studied. Suddenly, a thought struck Reeya. Could these be the missing *Panchatantra* tales?

Chapter 10
The manuscript

Reeya couldn't believe she was standing in the ancient library. Let alone looking at what might be the originals of her favourite fairy tales. She called for Mum to come and see the manuscript.

Mum pulled out some gloves from her tool bag. "We don't want the oils from our skin to stain the manuscripts," she explained. She put on the gloves before taking the manuscript from Reeya.

As Mum carefully examined the book, her eyes grew wider. After a few minutes, she laughed as if she'd just read a joke.

"I don't believe it! This is your favourite story, Reeya, the one about the boastful turtle! I'll send a sample to the lab to make sure. But if they authenticate this as the original *Panchatantra* manuscript, it's the find of the century!"

"Wow! That's incredible! But how did it end up here in Egypt?" Reeya asked. Then she remembered what Dad had said about sailors having to hand over their books. "Do you think the library took it from Vishnu when he sailed here from India? But why would he have had it in the first place?"

"Those are good questions," Mum said, still studying the manuscript. "Unless the library kept a record, it's hard to kno–" She gasped upon seeing something in the book. "*Kyaa*? I don't believe it. These say that Vishnu is the author!"

"Really?" Reeya swelled with joy at the thought that Vishnu had written her favourite stories.

"We need to let Dr Faisal know about this discovery right away," Mum said.

As Finlay's parents and Afifi photographed and catalogued the manuscripts, Mum and Dad took Reeya and Finlay back to the inn. There, her parents spoke to Dr Faisal in a private office, while Reeya and Finlay waited in reception.

Soon Elsie strolled in. When she saw them, she put her hands on her hips and glared.

"Well, what are you going to do about my rock? I want it back," she demanded.

Reeya sighed, pushed up her glasses, and looked Elsie squarely in the eyes. "First, it's not a rock. It's a scarab. Second, it doesn't belong to you. Third, we don't owe you anything. But to be fair, we'll make sure you get credit for finding the scarab when it's displayed in the museum. The sign could say, Discovered by Elsie–"

"Ooooh . . . I'll be famous!" Elsie interrupted as her eyes grew wide.

She ran off to tell her dad, who Reeya noticed was trying to eavesdrop on her parents and Dr Faisal. Reeya could hear Dr Faisal congratulating her parents. When Reeya caught Dr Acker's eye, he stood up straight, smoothed his clothes and scurried away with Elsie.

* * *

A few days later, after Reeya, Finlay and their parents moved back onto the houseboat, Mum got a phone call. After she'd hung up, she updated the group.

"That was Dr Faisal. The lab called and let her know that the manuscript is the original *Panchatantra*! It'll go to the national museum in India. The rest of the manuscripts and artefacts will stay in Egypt's museums."

The group cheered. Reeya smiled, knowing her favourite tales would return to their homeland.

Suddenly, a deep voice from the dock broke up their celebration. Dr Acker approached the boat with a strained smile.

"I believe congratulations are in order. Some of us must work for our success, but it appears you got lucky," Dr Acker said with a sarcastic chuckle that annoyed Reeya. "I'd like to offer my help with your valuable manuscripts. I can read Greek, Roman, ancient Egyptian, Sanskrit–"

"Uh, thank you," Dad interrupted. "We'll let you know if we need your help."

Dr Acker gave a brief nod and sulked away. Elsie followed him, throwing a sour look back at Reeya and Finlay.

Reeya just smiled. Not even the Ackers could ruin this happy day. Vishnu had been a twelve-year-old sailor from India, a hero and the author of one of the most important Sanskrit books of all time. The world had forgotten him for more than 2,000 years. But not anymore. Reeya would make sure of it.

She settled down in her deckchair to gaze out at the sea and think of new ideas to write in her notebook. She couldn't wait to create a new invention that might help her parents with their next discovery. Who knows? Maybe it could even help rewrite history.

Make your own roller transporter!

With a few simple materials, you can make your own transporter inspired by Reeya's invention! Ask an adult to help you build this fun rolling invention.

Materials needed:

- 8 empty toilet roll tubes
- heavy cardboard
- thin cardboard
- 8 paper straws
- 1 small cardboard box
- glue
- pencil
- ruler
- scissors

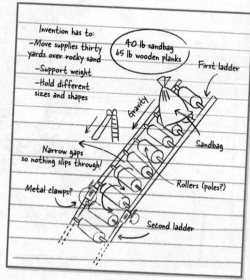

Invention has to:
- Move supplies thirty yards over rocky sand
- Support weight
- Hold different sizes and shapes

40 lb sandbag
65 lb wooden planks

First ladder

Gravity

Sandbag

Narrow gaps so nothing slips through!

Rollers (poles?)

Metal clamps?

Second ladder

What to do:

1. Trace 16 circles on the thin cardboard with a toilet roll tube. Then cut them out with scissors.

2. In the centre of each circle, make a hole to slide a straw through. Make sure the circles easily spin around the straw. If they don't, make the holes slightly larger. Then glue the circles to the ends of the toilet roll tubes. Let the glue dry.

3. Slide the straws through the tubes. Check that they spin freely. If not, make sure the holes are large enough and that the straw is straight.

4. Cut two strips of heavy cardboard 5 cm wide and 46 cm long.

5. Make eight marks in the centre of each cardboard strip spaced 5 cm apart. Make a hole at each mark large enough to slide a straw through.

6. With each roller, push the straw ends into the matching holes of each cardboard strip. Then glue the straws in place. Do not get any glue on the rollers. Let the glue dry.

7. Lean your roller transporter against the cardboard box. Place a lightweight object on the transporter and watch it roll to the bottom!

More about ancient India and ancient Egypt

♦ Historians believe India began trading goods with other civilizations as much as 5,000 years ago. Indian merchants probably sailed for several weeks to Egypt to trade goods. They sold goods such as spices, muslin fabric and semi-precious stones. They even sold animals such as monkeys, which people bought as pets.

♦ The Mouseion was founded in the 200s BC in Alexandria, Egypt. It was a research centre that contained the Great Library and many other features. Scholars travelled far to study there. The library had thousands of manuscripts from all over the world, including India.

♦ When sailors docked in Alexandria, they were required to hand over any books to the library to be copied. The library would give the copy to the owner and keep the original for its collection. The library caught on fire during a war in 48 BC. It's not known how much of the library or its collection was destroyed.

Papyrus

- Ancient Egyptians made their paper-like material from a plant called papyrus. They cut the plant into strips, which were laid out in layers, pressed together, and dried in the sun to make sheets. People dipped thin reeds or brushes in ink to write on the papyrus scrolls. Black ink was made from soot, water mixed with ash or burnt oil. Colourful minerals were crushed to make coloured ink.

- The *Panchatantra* tales were a set of animal fables written in Sanskrit between 100 BC and AD 500. Many scholars believe a teacher called Vishnu Sharma wrote the tales to help a king teach his three sons about good behaviour. While copies of the tales have been found, the originals are lost.

Talk about it

1. The sailor Vishnu was new to Egypt. How do you think he felt? Have you ever visited or lived somewhere new? Did others make you feel welcome?

2. If a person finds an artefact, do you think they should keep it or contact a museum instead? Why do you think this? Remember, in many places it's illegal to keep an artefact, especially if it's found on public land.

3. Elsie can be a bully. Why do you think she acts the way she does? How would you handle someone like Elsie? Make sure you tell a guardian or teacher if you are ever bullied. Bullying is never okay.

Write about it

1. Can you think of another invention that could have helped save the catacombs from flooding? Draw it out and label the parts. What does each part do? How do they all work together? Write out a plan for how to build the invention and explain how it works.

2. Imagine a merchant from India who sailed to ancient Egypt to trade goods such as spices or cloth. Write a short story about the merchant's journey and experiences in a strange country.

3. Scarabs are seals with a picture of a scarab beetle on one side. The other side is unique to the owner and may contain pictures, the owner's name, places, good wishes or other important information. If you had a scarab made for yourself, what would it say?

Glossary

Arabic main language of Egypt

bazaar street market full of shopping stalls

catacombs underground cemetery, usually consisting of tunnels and chambers with spaces to hold bodies

fez red felt hat with a flat top

hieroglyph picture or symbol used in the ancient Egyptian system of writing

hijab traditional scarf worn by Muslim women to cover their hair, necks and faces

papyrus paper-like writing material made from the papyrus plant, often used in ancient Egypt

scarab stone resembling a beetle, often used in ancient Egypt as a symbol or seal

tram public transport vehicle that travels on railway tracks on the street

viper snake that kills its prey with venom

Anita Nahta Amin

Anita Nahta Amin is a second generation Indian American and former information technology manager. She is the author of several fiction and non-fiction children's books. Her notebook is one of her most prized possessions, and she is always writing ideas in it.

Farimah Khavarinezhad

Farimah Khavarinezhad is a freelance illustrator currently based in Canada. She loves incorporating details into her illustrations, with warm and cosy colours. Her favourite thing about illustrating is that it is similar to magic. Illustrations bring characters and elements to life.

Marta Morado

Marta Dorado was born in Gijón, Spain, and raised in a nearby village. She later moved to Pamplona to attend university, where she still lives. Her childhood was surrounded by nature and close to the sea, which has strongly influenced her work.

Hiya, it's Reeya!

Read about all my adventures with my family and friends.

Reeya Rai and the King's Treasure

written by Anita Nahta Amin
Illustrated by Farimah Khavarinezhad

Reeya Rai and the Ivory Peacock

written by Anita Nahta Amin
Illustrated by Farimah Khavarinezhad

Reeya Rai and the Lost Library

written by Anita Nahta Amin
Illustrated by Farimah Khavarinezhad

Reeya Rai and the Secret Workshop

written by Anita Nahta Amin
Illustrated by Farimah Khavarinezhad

Hurry, before Elsie or her dad grabs them first!